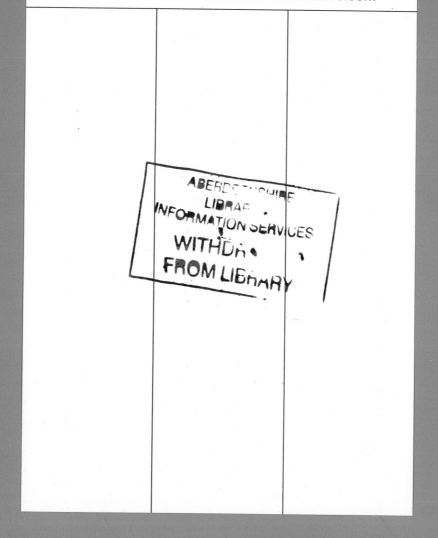

JP

To Sophie, George, Luca,
William and Rory

– Sian Tucker

A DAVID BENNETT BOOK

First published in the United Kingdom in 2003
by Chrysalis Children's Books,
The Chrysalis Building, Bramley Road
London W10 6SP

Illustrations copyright © 2003 Sian Tucker.

Sian Tucker asserts her moral right to be
identified as the illustrator of this work.

BRITISH LIBRARY CATALOGUING-IN-PUBLICATION DATA
A catalogue record for this book is available from the British Library.

ISBN 1 85602 482 2
Printed in Singapore

My First Book Of

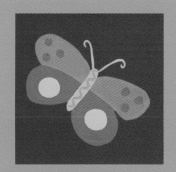

Numbers

Sian Tucker

Chrysalis Children's Books

One little dinosaur following his mummy.

1 2 3 4 5 6 7 8 9 10

How many spots can you count on his tummy?

11 12 13 14 15 16 17 18 19 20

Left shoe, right shoe - that makes two.

1 2 3 4 5 6 7 8 9 10

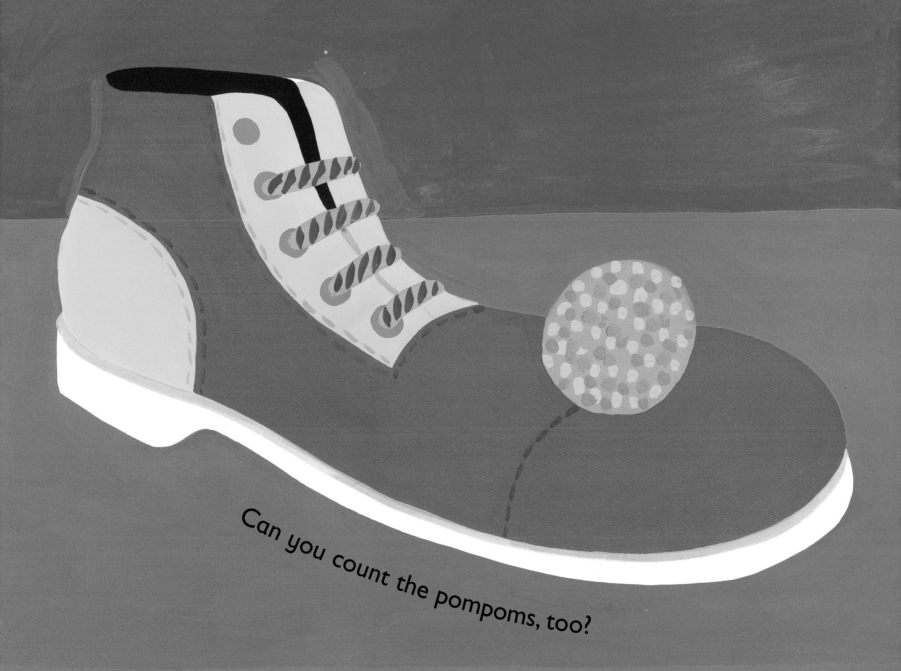

Can you count the pompoms, too?

11 12 13 14 15 16 17 18 19 20

Three warty witches, one, two, three.

1 2 3 4 5 6 7 8 9 10

How many broomsticks can you see?

11 12 13 14 15 16 17 18 19 20

Four knobbly planets far, far away.

1 2 3 4 5 6 7 8 9 10

How many aliens have come out to play?

11 12 13 14 15 16 17 18 19 20

Five happy snowmen having a ball.

1 2 3 4 5 6 7 8 9 10

How many snowflakes have started to fall?

11 12 13 14 15 16 17 18 19 20

Can you count the mermaids – splish, splash, splish –

1 2 3 4 5 6 7 8 9 10

as they swim in the sea with six stripy fish?

11 12 13 14 15 16 17 18 19 20

Seven jolly cowboys at a wild-west rodeo.

1 2 3 4 5 6 7 8 9 10

How many lassos are they ready to throw?

11 12 13 14 15 16 17 18 19 20

Eight pretty butterflies flitting through the trees.

1 2 3 4 5 6 7 8 9 10

Can you count the flowers swaying in the breeze?

11 12 13 14 15 16 17 18 19 20

Nine spooky ghosts floating in the gloom.

1 2 3 4 5 6 7 8 9 10

Can you count the cobwebs hanging in the room?

11 12 13 14 15 16 17 18 19 20

Eleven busy elves working away.

How many toys have they finished today?

11 12 13 14 15 16 17 18 19 20

Twelve bouncy dogs bounding into view.

1 2 3 4 5 6 7 8 9 10

How many bones do they have to chew?

11 **12** 13 14 15 16 17 18 19 20

Thirteen cheery children coming round the bend.

How many wheels can you count from end to end?

11 **12** **13** 14 15 16 17 18 19 20

Fourteen smiley sailors rowing to the shore.

1 2 3 4 5 6 7 8 9 10

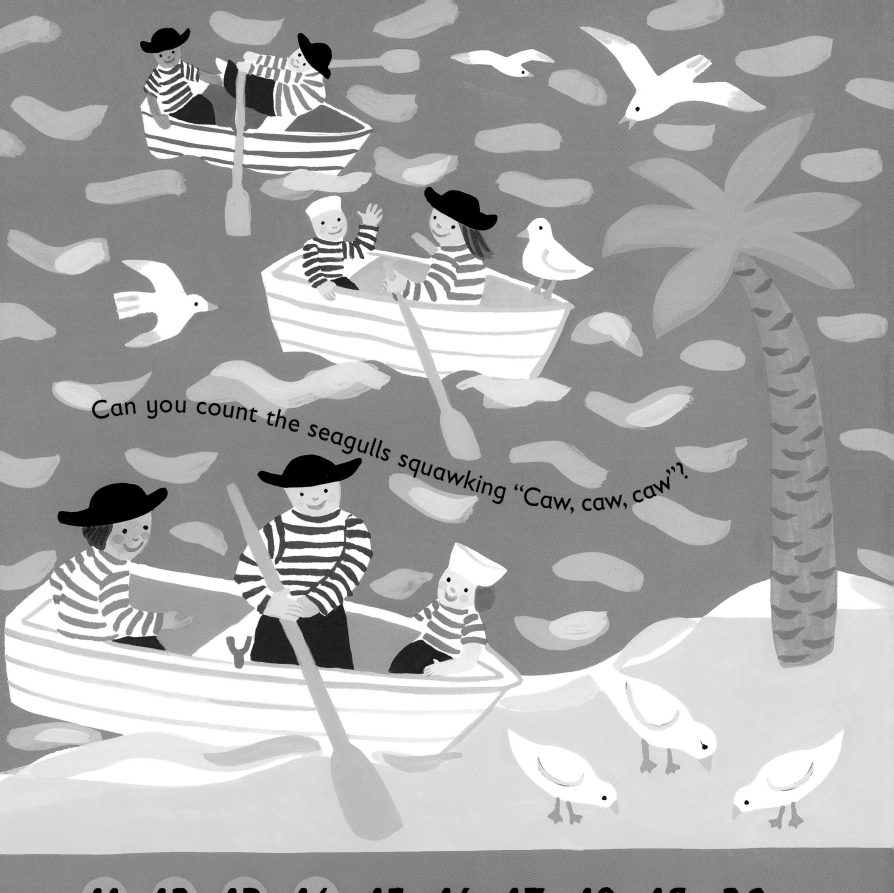

Can you count the seagulls squawking "Caw, caw, caw"?

11 12 13 14 15 16 17 18 19 20

Fifteen ballet dancers twirling gracefully.

1 2 3 4 5 6 7 8 9 10

How many ribbons can you see?

11 12 13 14 15 16 17 18 19 20

Sixteen clowns at a birthday surprise.

1 2 3 4 5 6 7 8 9 10

Can you count their custard pies?

11 12 13 14 15 16 17 18 19 20

Seventeen hearts on a queen's velvet gown.

Can you count the jewels that sparkle in her crown?

1 2 3 4 5 6 7 8 9 10

11 **12** **13** **14** **15** **16** **17** 18 19 20

Eighteen little buggies on a funfair ride.

Can you count the children as they swoosh down the slide?

11 12 13 14 15 16 17 18 19 20

Nineteen hot-air balloons drifting slowly by.

1 2 3 4 5 6 7 8 9 10

How many clouds can you see in the sky?

11 **12** **13** **14** **15** **16** **17** **18** **19** **20**

Twenty sparkling stars when it's time to go to bed.

1 2 3 4 5 6 7 8 9 10

How many rockets are zooming overhead?

11 12 13 14 15 16 17 18 19 20